FOR CADEN AND TORIN — AT
THE END OF THE DAY, I'LL
ALWAYS BE THERE FOR YOU.
JN

FOR ANDREA, WHO TURNS
EVERY PLACE INTO A HOME.
LA

CATERPILLAR BOOKS
An imprint of Little Tiger Group
1 The Coda Centre, 189 Munster Road, London SW6 6AW
www.littletiger.co.uk • First published in Great Britain 2017
Text copyright © Jeff Norton 2017
Illustrations copyright © Leo Antolini 2017
All rights reserved • ISBN: 978-1-84857-588-2
Printed in China • CPB/1800/0654/0417
2 4 6 8 10 9 7 5 3 1

ANA is a slithering, athletic, always-on-the-move anaconda. The spawn of city-swallowing mega-snakes, she is more interested in athletics than swallowing cities. She also has a competitive streak.

SHERPA is a thrill-seeking Yeti. Happier in the mountains than in the city, she has an intrepid spirit for exploring the natural world. She can commune with animals, but often gets lost in translation. She wears a hiker's backpack and is always prepared for adventure – even if the adventure is just snack-time.

TERRY is a daydreaming pterodactyl who's still learning to fly – more often falling than flying. But he doesn't let that spoil his unfailing good humour – and he certainly won't stop trying to fly!

FARI AND RAFI are gorilla twins, distinguished only by their green and purple electric collars. Fari is rough and tumble. She's always up for a stomp, while Rafi would rather play tea parties with his pet human doll, Fay.

WRITTEN BY
JEFF NORTON

PICTURES BY
LEO ANTOLINI

STOMP
SCHOOL

KRAKE is a one-squid accidental demolition crew. With tentacles flailing, he's literally all over the place! He tries to do eight things at once and can't keep himself straight, relying on Sherpa or Rikki to untangle him.

DRAGLO the dragon is the one kaiju at nursery who pines for his nest-parents. Rikki and the group try to cheer him up, but he suffers from a constant cold, sniffling and sneezing... blowing fire!

LUPA is not so much a werewolf as a wherewolf: a wolf with a terrible sense of direction. The cheeky troublemaker of the class, she loves to jump and howl and sing.

RIKKI is a sensitive but intrepid lil' kaiju with a big heart and a talent for building the best cities. In human years, he is a precocious three and a half. He's wide-eyed and curious about the world, but his enthusiasm leads him to leap before he looks.

TORIK is a toddler kaiju who embraces his terrible twos. He can talk, but prefers to growl. He throws his food, demands a lot of attention, and wrecks Rikki's toys. A born stomper!

Rikki was building his biggest, best city ever.

He couldn't wait to show his daddy.

"Now, how will I show Daddy what I built?"

Great stomping, kaiju.

"I think you're ready for Stomp School," called Rikki's dad.

Rikki was so upset that he slammed his foot down.

...and **SMASHED**

the city to pieces.

Rikki just wanted to go
home to his building bricks.

Miss Bronte asked the class,
"What shall we play today?"

"Lets build the
biggest, best city
ever," cried Rikki.

The kaiju kids all cheered.

"Brilliant building," said Miss Bronte.

"Now, it's time to..."

They built for hours
without stopping.*

* except for snacks, toilet, lunch, toilet,
nap, toilet and more snacks.

STOMP! CRUSH!
SMASH!
STOMP!

NOOO!

"But then how will I show my daddy what I built?" cried Rikki.

Rikki was so upset that he
SLAMMED HIS FOOT DOWN.

"Great stomping, kaiju,"
said Miss Bronte.

"But before we stomp, it's time to paint,
so you can show everyone what you built."

Rikki painted his best city ever.

Finally,
Rikki was
ready to

RAMP

They # STOMPED

They

CRUSHED

They

BASHED

Just then, Rikki's dad arrived to take him home.

"Look Daddy, see what I built?"

"It's your biggest, best city ever," beamed Rikki's daddy.

The family set off for home.

"Stomp School is awesome!
Can I go back tomorrow?"

STOMP SCHOOL